Eyes That See Do Not Grow Old

GUY A. ZONA

A TOUCHSTONE BOOK
Published by Simon & Schuster
NEW YORK   LONDON   TORONTO   SYDNEY

TOUCHSTONE
Rockefeller Center
1230 Avenue of the Americas
New York, NY 10020

TOUCHSTONE and colophon are registered trademarks
of Simon & Schuster Inc.

Designed by Irving Perkins Associates

Manufactured in the United States of America

3   5   7   9   10   8   6   4

Library of Congress Cataloging-in-Publication Data
Zona, Guy A.
Eyes that see do not grow old : the proverbs of Mexico,
Central and South America / Guy A. Zona
p.   cm.
"A Touchstone book."
1. Proverbs, Spanish—Latin America.   I. Title
PN6495.L29Z66   1996
398.9'61'098—dc20   95-50136
CIP
ISBN-13: 978-0-684-80018-9
ISBN-10:   0-684-80018-7

Contributing Countries

ARGENTINA	DOMINICAN REPUBLIC	PANAMA
BOLIVIA	ECUADOR	PARAGUAY
CHILE	GUATEMALA	PERU
COLOMBIA	HONDURAS	PUERTO RICO
COSTA RICA	MEXICO	URUGUAY
CUBA	NICARAGUA	VENEZUELA

Introduction

"It is said best when it is said through a proverb." Such is the belief of most of the citizens of the Spanish-speaking countries of Mexico and Central and South America, just as it is in many other cultures around the world. The strong use of figurative language by these serene and often light-hearted people delivers cameolike images of profound morality and exquisite kindness. Latino proverbs have a pleasant and picturesque way of contributing toward the understanding and point of view from which the family of mankind looks upon complexities of human life.

The proverbs living on the lips of the Latino people, though they may be brief, speak of lengthy wisdom. They are an artistic art form firmly steeped in philosophic treasures. Often deeply rooted in religious content, they speak of happiness and misery, sorrow and joy, riches and poverty, honor and disgrace, beauty and ugliness, power and weakness, greatness and smallness, as well as youth and old age, love and hatred, death and future life. Latino proverbs have a strong inclination toward training and an understanding of the philosophy of life. They adequately express judgments and evaluations based on life's many and varied experiences. Within the wide scope of these proverbs there may be found an almost complete chart of human nature as the Latino people perceive it to be.

In pondering the proverbs of the Latino people one will frequently find expressions of universally admitted truths. They render such a beautifully artistic art form that they can readily be found in various forms of formal literature.

It is with much pride and a true sense of sharing that this selection of choice proverbs is presented.

Guy A. Zona

The night is a cloak for sinners.

PUERTO RICO

❖

There is never wanting an excuse for drinking.

CUBA

❖

The needle knows what it sews and the thimble what it pushes.

COLOMBIA

❖

Of the doctor, the poet, and the fool we all have a small portion.

MEXICO

❖

A hundred years of war and not one day of fighting.

❖

There is no better friend than a burden.

Colombia

❖

A good surgeon must have a hawk's eye, a lion's heart, and a woman's hand.

Dominican Republic

❖

Rocking chairs make long-tailed cats uneasy.

Mexico

❖

Some are thought good and some bad, and both are wronged.

CUBA

❖

A false friend's tongue is sharper than a knife.

ARGENTINA

❖

The idle remarks of the rich are taken as maxims of wisdom by the poor.

ECUADOR

❖

Every time one laughs a nail is removed from one's coffin.

HONDURAS

❖

That which does not reach a man reaches his reputation.
MEXICO

❖

Eyes that see do not grow old.
NICARAGUA

❖

Words of the mouth are like a stone in a sling.
MEXICO

❖

He who commits many faults is never without an excuse.
PARAGUAY

❖

A word and a stone once thrown away cannot be returned.
MEXICO

Seven sons of one mother and each one of a different mind.

CUBA

❖

The child weeps for its good and the old man for his ill.

PERU

❖

There is a remedy for all things except death.

PUERTO RICO

❖

Riches are the baggage of fortune.

PUERTO RICO

❖

He who does not venture has no luck.

MEXICO

With the rod with which you measure, you will be measured.

❖

The hypocrite is known by his actions, not by his clothes.

❖

Hope doesn't fatten but it supports.

❖

For a new sin, a new penance.

❖

He who has servants has unavoidable enemies.

PUERTO RICO

❖

It is God that gave us increase.

CUBA

❖

The tongue touches the tooth that aches.

PUERTO RICO

❖

That which is a sin in others is a virtue in ourselves.

CHILE

❖

Fortune favors the brave.

MEXICO

A beard well lathered is half shaved.

PUERTO RICO

❖

He who talks much errs much.

MEXICO

❖

One man's meat is another man's poison.

PUERTO RICO

❖

We like the treason, but not the traitor.

PUERTO RICO

❖

From the tree of silence hangs the fruit of tranquillity.

PERU

Gratitude is the least of virtues; ingratitude is the worst of vices.

PARAGUAY

❖

Every owl to its own olive tree.

CUBA

❖

Good silence is called holiness.

PANAMA

❖

The throat must pay for what the tongue may say.

MEXICO

❖

Eat the bread of the man you hate and also of him you love.

PUERTO RICO

❖

To flee and to run are not the same thing.

NICARAGUA

❖

Grief shared is half grief; joy shared is double joy.

HONDURAS

❖

A good friend is better than a near relation.

ARGENTINA

❖

One never falls but on the side toward which one leans.

ECUADOR

Letters without virtue are pearls on a dung hill.

ARGENTINA

❖

Scanty means are severe judges.

PUERTO RICO

❖

Wounds from the knife are healed, but not those from the tongue.

MEXICO

❖

The voice of the people is the voice of God.

ARGENTINA

❖

When God gives the light of day, it is for all.

CUBA

❖

Wheat is cleansed by the wind and vice by punishment.

ARGENTINA

❖

There is no choosing between two things of no value.

MEXICO

❖

Lord save me from my friends, from my enemies I shall guard myself.

CUBA

❖

With patience and saliva the elephant swallows an ant.

COLOMBIA

❖

The way of this world is to praise dead saints and persecute living ones.

DOMINICAN REPUBLIC

❖

The dog in the manger won't eat the oats or let anyone else eat them.

COLOMBIA

❖

The new pleases and the old satisfies.

CUBA

Compliments between intimate friends are dispensed with.

ARGENTINA

❖

Manners and money make sons gentlemen.

ECUADOR

❖

One washes the body in vain if one does not wash the soul.

CUBA

❖

You may believe every good report of a grateful man.

GUATEMALA

❖

It's easy to trust a cat once you put the cream out of reach.

MEXICO

He who follows his own advice must take the consequences.

MEXICO

❖

He who excuses himself without being accused makes his guilt known.

HONDURAS

❖

Each one scratches himself with his own nails.

MEXICO

❖

Everyone knows where his own shoe pinches him.

MEXICO

It is not enough for a man to know how to ride, he must also know how to fall.

PUERTO RICO

❖

The vulgar keep no account of your hits, but of your misses.

PARAGUAY

❖

Love looks through spectacles that make copper look like gold, poverty like riches, and tears like pearls.

PERU

❖

Let him who knows the instrument play upon it.

CUBA

Let him attack who will; the strong wait.

MEXICO

❖

To "Get out of my house" or "What do you want with my wife?" there is no answer.

BOLIVIA

❖

He who does not praise a thing is he who buys it.

MEXICO

❖

Every land fosters its own art.

CHILE

❖

A man forewarned is equal to two.

MEXICO

❖

A good beginning is half the work done.

PUERTO RICO

❖

A rolling stone never gathers moss.

PUERTO RICO

❖

The clown is best in his own country, and the gentleman anywhere.

MEXICO

❖

He who assists everybody assists nobody.

MEXICO

❖

He who overcomes his passions overcomes his greatest enemies.

COLOMBIA

❖

Works, and not words, are the proofs of love.

MEXICO

❖

Idleness is the mother of vice.

PUERTO RICO

❖

If you would be respected in company, seek the society of your equals, and not of your superiors.

CUBA

❖

See and believe, and in order not to make a mistake, touch.

COLOMBIA

❖

He who speaks sows, and he who listens harvests.

ARGENTINA

❖

Never show your wounded finger to the world.

COSTA RICA

❖

Virtues all agree, but vices fight one another.

ARGENTINA

❖

That which goes not away in tears goes away in sighs.

CUBA

❖

Art is better than strength.

PUERTO RICO

❖

He who does not honor his wife dishonors himself.

MEXICO

❖

Two in harmony are in God's company.

ARGENTINA

Nothing is so burdensome as a secret.

COLOMBIA

❖

When vices forsake us, we flatter ourselves that it is we
who forsake them.

CUBA

❖

Two sparrows upon one ear of corn cannot agree.

PUERTO RICO

❖

You must not tell all that you know, nor judge all that you
see, if you would live in peace.

MEXICO

❖

If fate throws a knife at you, there are two ways of catching it: by the blade or by the handle.

DOMINICAN REPUBLIC

❖

A good man finds his native soil in every country.

MEXICO

❖

Instruction in youth is like engraving in stones.

COLOMBIA

❖

Where the sun doesn't enter the doctor does.

CUBA

❖

Let us, independent of fathers and grandfathers, be good for our own sake.

PUERTO RICO

❖

Tell me what company you keep and I will tell you who you are.

CUBA

❖

The eye of the master fattens the horse.

GUATEMALA

❖

Cheese, wine, and a friend must be old to be good.

CUBA

❖

Good news is rumored and bad news flies.

HONDURAS

❖

Faces of men we see, but not their hearts.

CUBA

❖

Break the leg of a bad habit.

PUERTO RICO

❖

A lie runs until it is overtaken by truth.

CUBA

❖

Speak plain; call bread, bread, and wine, wine.

MEXICO

Rare is the person who can weigh the faults of another without putting his thumb on the scales.

PARAGUAY

❖

He who punishes one chastises a hundred.

MEXICO

❖

I will do anything, but will not take it upon myself to guard a house with two doors.

PUERTO RICO

❖

He who makes more of you than usual either designs to cheat you or wants your assistance.

MEXICO

If I listen I have the advantage, if I speak the others have it.

PERU

❖

He who tells the truth doesn't sin, but he causes many inconveniences.

CUBA

❖

See before you tie how you can untie.

PUERTO RICO

❖

Ten who shout obtain much more than ten who remain silent.

MEXICO

❖

Slow and sure go far, and the more haste, the worse speed.

PUERTO RICO

❖

Pay what you owe and you will know what you are worth.

MEXICO

❖

He loses his thanks who promises and delays.

MEXICO

❖

If you would have good fame, do not let the sun shine upon you in bed.

PUERTO RICO

❖

Gifts break rocks and melt hearts.

❖

A good friend will fit you like ring to finger.

VENEZUELA

❖

You cannot distinguish between a drunken man and a mad
man until they have slept.

COLOMBIA

❖

Time never respects what is done with its aid.

PUERTO RICO

❖

Let not the tongue speak what the head may have to pay for.

MEXICO

❖

He bears a burning coal in his bosom who brings up another's son.

ARGENTINA

❖

Even if your pockets are empty, see that your hat is on straight.

COLOMBIA

❖

He who goes the wrong road must go the journey twice over.

COSTA RICA

Brief confrontations make long friends.

CUBA

❖

To have companions in our labors lightens our toil.

PUERTO RICO

❖

Better to be the pot than the lid.

COLOMBIA

❖

If you return an ass's kicks, most of the pain is yours.

CUBA

❖

The rat that knows but one hole is soon caught by the cat.

MEXICO

The devil always paints himself black, but we always see him rose-colored.

DOMINICAN REPUBLIC

❖

Nobility exists in virtue.

ARGENTINA

❖

The monkey knows onto which tree to climb.

COLOMBIA

❖

A house that has neither a dog nor cat is the house of a rogue.

CUBA

❖

Clear accounts and thick chocolate.

ARGENTINA

❖

Coffee from the top of the cup and chocolate from the bottom.

CUBA

❖

Since I injured you, I have never liked you.

PUERTO RICO

❖

To a good listener only a few words are needed.

ECUADOR

❖

He who avoids the temptations, avoids the sin.

GUATEMALA

❖

Each one knows with how many threads he sews.

MEXICO

❖

Great deeds are reserved for great men.

MEXICO

❖

That which is left to time remains with time.

PUERTO RICO

❖

A habitual drunkard has never a sufficiency of either wine or water.

CUBA

❖

He who is not of the water swims well.

MEXICO

❖

Jovial companions make this dull life tolerable.

CUBA

❖

Such a question you ask, such an answer you will receive.

PUERTO RICO

❖

You can't call a cat honest if the meat is out of reach.

MEXICO

❖

Youth is intoxication without wine; old age, wine without intoxication.

PERU

❖

Of sons and friends, many are too few.

CUBA

❖

No wedding without singing, nor a burial without weeping.

PUERTO RICO

❖

Love flies away and the pain remains.

BOLIVIA

❖

When you have spoken of your kindred, go and refresh
yourself.

CUBA

❖

A friar who asks alms for God's sake begs for two.

PUERTO RICO

❖

He who spits in the air will have it fall back on his face.

MEXICO

❖

He who goes away without being turned out comes back without being called.

CHILE

❖

The bread of your own home is always good.

CUBA

❖

He who has enemies, let him not sleep.

PUERTO RICO

❖

He who keeps a secret prevents much mischief.

MEXICO

❖

No one has done good who has not suffered disillusion-ment.

CHILE

❖

A little frightens and much softens.

PUERTO RICO

❖

When God wills, it rains with every wind.

CUBA

❖

One devil that is known is better than twenty to be known.

PUERTO RICO

❖

A "no" in time is better than a late "yes."
URUGUAY

❖

He who loiters hears ill spoken of himself.
MEXICO

❖

God punishes, but not with a rod.
CUBA

❖

A good companion should have good company.
VENEZUELA

❖

He who loves you will make you weep.
ARGENTINA

The eating will give you the appetite.

COLOMBIA

❖

Wine like a king, and water like an ox.

CUBA

❖

He who has a hundred and one pesos, and owes a hundred and two, let him commend himself to God.

MEXICO

❖

When you mourn, you cannot sing; when you sing, you cannot mourn.

ARGENTINA

❖

Power has no friends, envy has no rest, and crime has no satisfaction.

DOMINICAN REPUBLIC

❖

The cat that stays at home catches the most mice.

CUBA

❖

Where there is no want of will, there will be no want of opportunity.

MEXICO

❖

Pray to God and hammer away.

PUERTO RICO

❖

What is lost today may not be gained tomorrow.

CUBA

❖

He who has no malice fears no malice.

ARGENTINA

❖

There is no avenging yourself upon a rich man.

ECUADOR

❖

The friend who will not lend, and the knife that will not
cut: if you lose them it is of little consequence.

CUBA

❖

When the devil prays, he wishes to deceive you.

PUERTO RICO

❖

He who eats his cock alone saddles his horse alone.

MEXICO

❖

When one is helping another, both gain in strength.

ECUADOR

❖

It is much better to eat beans in peace than fowl in disquiet.

GUATEMALA

❖

He who pays punctually has no difficulty about pledges.
MEXICO

❖

In every path there is a dirty place.
NICARAGUA

❖

The tongue slow and the eyes quick.
MEXICO

❖

A resolute heart will not be advised.
CUBA

❖

The lance never blunted the pen, nor the pen the lance.
NICARAGUA

Believe only half of what you see and nothing of what you are told.

❖

Until death, all is life.

❖

Though you possess prudence, old man, do not despise advice.

❖

Every fool is pleased with his own blunder.

❖

Money is not advice.

PERU

❖

Silence was never written down.

PUERTO RICO

❖

From the rich man to the proud one, there is not a palm's length.

MEXICO

❖

He loves you well who makes you weep.

BOLIVIA

❖

What may not happen in a year may happen in an instant.

PUERTO RICO

❖

He who has no shame has no conscience.

MEXICO

❖

Where distrust enters, love is no more than a boy.

CHILE

❖

Every sheep hangs by its own foot.

MEXICO

❖

He who seeks work has food in the embers.

PUERTO RICO

Although a monkey be dressed in silk, she is still a monkey.

MEXICO

❖

One man driven by distress does as much as thirty.

MEXICO

❖

Many are the roads by which God brings his own to heaven.

VENEZUELA

❖

He is not to blame who does his duty.

MEXICO

❖

Let those Pater Nosters be for your own soul.

❖

He who shows a passion tells his enemy where he may hit him.

COLOMBIA

❖

God sends the cold to each one according to his clothes.

ARGENTINA

❖

Listen to what they say of others and you will know what they say of you.

CUBA

❖

A jealous lover makes an indifferent husband.

PUERTO RICO

❖

A woman and glass are always in danger.

MEXICO

❖

Sow corn in clay, and plant vines in gravel.

COSTA RICA

❖

The sleeping shrimp is carried away by the tide.

COLOMBIA

❖

Sense comes with age.

CUBA

The work of many is the work of none.

PUERTO RICO

❖

A secret between two is God's secret; a secret between three is known to all.

MEXICO

❖

Him who does not speak God does not hear.

VENEZUELA

❖

He who recognizes his folly is on the road to wisdom.

COLOMBIA

❖

There is a great distance between said and done.

PUERTO RICO

❖

He who ties well unties well.

MEXICO

❖

Worth makes the man, and want of it the fellow.

MEXICO

❖

That which is done at night appears in the day.

URUGUAY

❖

He who doesn't look ahead remains behind.

MEXICO

He who abandons his family, God forsakes him.

VENEZUELA

❖

Don't be like the shadow: a constant companion, yet not a comrade.

DOMINICAN REPUBLIC

❖

He who sows wind reaps a tempest.

CUBA

❖

An open door tempts even a saint.

ECUADOR

❖

Give your love to your wife and your secret to your mother.

GUATEMALA

❖

Faults never fall to the ground.

HONDURAS

❖

Taste is in variety, variety in taste.

NICARAGUA

❖

It is in one's work that we discover love and faith.

MEXICO

❖

Eyes to see with, ears to hear with, and a mouth to keep silence.

PARAGUAY

❖

Love and prudence are absolutely incompatible.

BOLIVIA

❖

The dog saw himself in velvet breeches and did not know his old companion.

CUBA

❖

To the hungry man no bread is bad.

MEXICO

❖

May the sun set on me where my love dwells.

BOLIVIA

❖

Words should be weighed, not counted.

PUERTO RICO

❖

When one will not, two cannot quarrel.

COLOMBIA

❖

The darts of love are blunted by the modesty of maidens.

MEXICO

❖

Even the best cloth has an uneven thread.

HONDURAS

Giving alms never empties the purse.

COSTA RICA

❖

To the satiated bird, cherries taste bitter.

MEXICO

❖

The coal that has been an ember is easily rekindled.

URUGUAY

❖

Join with good men, and you will be one of them.

VENEZUELA

❖

One swallow does not make a summer.

DOMINICAN REPUBLIC

Kittens are a child's instrument for happiness.
CUBA

❖

A weapon is an enemy even to its owner.
GUATEMALA

❖

He who covers you discovers you.
MEXICO

❖

The lazy servant, to save going one step, goes eight.
NICARAGUA

❖

Truth is God's daughter.
PUERTO RICO

Woman is like your shadow: follow her, she flies; fly from her, she follows.

❖

The better the day the better the deed.

❖

He who gives quickly gives twice.

❖

God made us and we wonder at it.

❖

Blood is inherited and virtue is acquired.

VENEZUELA

❖

Words and feathers are carried away by the wind.

MEXICO

❖

An oak is not felled at one blow.

PUERTO RICO

❖

Advice is a stranger: if welcome, he stays for the night; if not welcome, he returns home the same day.

DOMINICAN REPUBLIC

❖

It takes two people to make one person angry.

ECUADOR

❖

In lying and eating fish, much care is needed.

CUBA

❖

That which is said at the table should be wrapped up in the tablecloth.

GUATEMALA

❖

Everything can be cured but foolishness.

PARAGUAY

❖

He who has money and bread may choose with whom to be a father-in-law.

PERU

❖

Who gossips to you will gossip of you.

PUERTO RICO

❖

He who denies the cat skimmed milk will give the mice the cream.

MEXICO

❖

He ought to be silent who gave, and let him speak who received.

ARGENTINA

When the bulls fight, it is bad for the branches.

HONDURAS

❖

The bad action remains with him who does it.

ARGENTINA

❖

He who has a trade may travel everywhere.

PUERTO RICO

❖

He who doesn't know is like him who doesn't see.

COLOMBIA

❖

When the cat is full, the milk tastes sour.

ARGENTINA

He who has a tail of straw should not go near the fire.

COLOMBIA

❖

He who knows nothing neither doubts nor fears anything.

MEXICO

❖

We are bound to forgive an enemy, we are not bound to trust him.

VENEZUELA

❖

Absence is the enemy of love, as the distance is from the eyes, so it is from the heart.

DOMINICAN REPUBLIC

❖

The strong forgive, the weak remember.

ECUADOR

❖

Every peddler praises his needles.

PARAGUAY

❖

Do not fear a stain that disappears with water.

PUERTO RICO

❖

What is much desired is not believed when it comes.

ARGENTINA

❖

What heaven ordains must be fulfilled on earth.

COLOMBIA

Between the beginning and the end there is always a middle.
MEXICO

❖

The good tree takes up one span, and yields five.
URUGUAY

❖

One sword keeps another in its scabbard.
VENEZUELA

❖

The eyes believe their own evidence, the ears that of others.
VENEZUELA

❖

The fear of the Lord is the beginning of wisdom.
CHILE

Time is the discoverer of all things.

DOMINICAN REPUBLIC

❖

He who sings frightens away his ills.

COLOMBIA

❖

The slanderer kills a thousand times; the assassin but once.

ECUADOR

❖

They who are in love think that other people's eyes are out.

BOLIVIA

❖

Friends in the marketplace are better than money in the chest.

❖

Gold, when beaten, shines.

❖

God puts food into clean hands.

❖

He who sows hopes in God.

❖

Perseverance kills the game and gains reward.

HONDURAS

❖

He who becomes irritated has twofold work: to be irritated and to be quit of his irritation.

COSTA RICA

❖

Beggars must not be choosers.

URUGUAY

❖

Proverbs in conversation are torches in darkness.

VENEZUELA

❖

A good dog deserves a good bone.

CHILE

❖

We must suit our behavior to the occasion.

COLOMBIA

❖

The pot that belongs to many is ill stirred and worse boiled.

ECUADOR

❖

May a bad oath fall upon a stone.

NICARAGUA

❖

Hide mends itself, but cloth has to be mended.

PANAMA

❖

A miser's money goes twice on the road.

PERU

❖

Tomorrow is often the busiest day of the week.

PUERTO RICO

❖

One door is shut, but a thousand are open.

ARGENTINA

❖

Envy shoots at others and wounds herself.

COSTA RICA

Find as much love as was given by your father and mother many times.

URUGUAY

❖

Treat the lesser as you would have the greater treat you.

VENEZUELA

❖

He who despises the little will soon weep for the much.

CHILE

❖

It is other people's burdens that kill the ass.

DOMINICAN REPUBLIC

❖

A love that can last forever takes but a second to come about.

CUBA

❖

He who errs and repents recommends himself to God.

COLOMBIA

❖

The master's foot is manure to the estate.

GUATEMALA

❖

Let him be wretched who thinks himself so.

MEXICO

❖

There are many things too bad for blessing and too good for cursing.

NICARAGUA

❖

The devil lurks even behind the cross.

PANAMA

❖

A man knows his companion in a long journey and a small inn.

BOLIVIA

❖

Fortune and olives are alike, sometimes a man has an abundance and other times not any.

PERU

There is no price for good advice.

PUERTO RICO

❖

Great expectations are better than poor possessions.

ARGENTINA

❖

Could everything be done twice, everything would be done better.

COSTA RICA

❖

Buckets of a well, those that come up full, go down empty.

URUGUAY

❖

Forgiveness is perfect only when the sin is not remembered.

VENEZUELA

❖

Where there is much love, there is usually but little boldness.

CHILE

❖

Honey is not for the ass's mouth.

DOMINICAN REPUBLIC

❖

The golden ass passes everywhere.

CUBA

❖

He preaches well who lives well.

COLOMBIA

❖

There is no secret that sooner or later will not be revealed.

ECUADOR

❖

Bad cloth discovers the thread.

GUATEMALA

❖

Where the cat caught a mouse she'll mouse again.

MEXICO

❖

It takes two to make a quarrel but only one to end it.

NICARAGUA

Half an orange tastes as sweet as a whole one.
PANAMA

❖

A friend in prosperity changes like the wind.
BOLIVIA

❖

Wind and good luck are seldom lasting.
PERU

❖

Poverty does not destroy virtue nor wealth bestow it.
COLOMBIA

❖

The day after is the pupil of the day before.
PUERTO RICO

Ingratitude is the child of pride.

ARGENTINA

❖

One "Take this" is worth more than two "I will give."

COSTA RICA

❖

Don't take every ill to the doctor, or every quarrel to the lawyer, or every thirst to the tavern.

URUGUAY

❖

God permits, but not forever.

CHILE

❖

He who has a son grown up should not call another a thief.

VENEZUELA

❖

There is no redemption in hell.

DOMINICAN REPUBLIC

❖

When money speaks, the rest are silent.

CUBA

❖

Joy lasts but a short time in a gamester's house.

COLOMBIA

❖

A man without honor is worse than dead.

ARGENTINA

❖

One person alone neither sings nor cries.

COSTA RICA

❖

Not with whom you are bred, but with whom you are fed.

VENEZUELA

❖

It is God who cures, and the physician gets the money.

CHILE

❖

The ant that grew wings grew them to his own destruction.

DOMINICAN REPUBLIC

Who has much on earth will have little in heaven.

CUBA

❖

Argue obstinately, but do not lay a wager.

COLOMBIA

❖

There can be no true pleasantry without discretion.

ECUADOR

❖

The deepest waters make the least noise.

GUATEMALA

❖

The lap of its owner is security enough for a cat.

MEXICO

There's nobody can prevent you getting into heaven, but there's many always ready to give you a shove into hell.

NICARAGUA

❖

Halfway is twelve miles when you have fourteen miles to go.

PANAMA

❖

Your best friend is a mirror.

BOLIVIA

❖

Diligence is the mother of good fortune.

PERU

❖

Politeness is to goodness what words are to thought.

COLOMBIA

❖

Love is deeds and not fine phrases.

PUERTO RICO

❖

He who lets one wait counts by seconds; he who has to wait counts in hours.

ARGENTINA

❖

The mother-in-law does not remember she was a daughter-in-law.

VENEZUELA

❖

The God who gives the wound gives also the medicine.
CHILE

❖

How can those be trusted who know not how to blush?
CUBA

❖

He who gives bread to a strange dog loses both his bread
and the dog.
COLOMBIA

❖

No man can serve two masters.
ECUADOR

❖

Old reckonings cause new quarrels.

GUATEMALA

❖

He who falls today may rise tomorrow.

MEXICO

❖

Renounce a friend who covers you with his wings and destroys you with his beak.

NICARAGUA

❖

A proverb is to speech what salt is to food.

PANAMA

❖

When the head aches, all the members suffer.

PERU

❖

The edifice of hate is built upon the stone of affronts.

COLOMBIA

❖

The deceiver, like the bee, has bone in his mouth and gall in his tail.

PUERTO RICO

❖

They are rich who have many friends.

COSTA RICA

❖

If you would be a good judge, pay attention to what everyone says.

MEXICO

❖

What I can see with my eyes I can point to with my finger.

DOMINICAN REPUBLIC

❖

A woman's honor consists in the good opinion the world has of her.

CUBA

❖

In eating and scratching everything is in the beginning.

COLOMBIA

❖

He who does not go to sea knows not how to pray.

ECUADOR

❖

Get a good name and go to sleep.

GUATEMALA

❖

The bowman who is a bad marksman has a lie ready.

MEXICO

❖

The evil that issues from your mouth falls into your bosom.

PUERTO RICO

❖

Those whom you wound with the mouth you must heal with the mouth.

COLOMBIA

❖

Secret joy is like a candle extinguished.

NICARAGUA

❖

Among the weak the strongest is the one who doesn't forget his weakness.

PANAMA

❖

One grain doesn't fill a granary, but it helps its companion.

BOLIVIA

❖

Pay what you owe and you will be cured of your complaint.

PERU

❖

A learned man is twice born.

ARGENTINA

❖

Each of us bears his friend and his enemy within himself.

COSTA RICA

❖

The dog that has his bitch in town never barks well.

MEXICO

❖

The wrath of brothers is the wrath of devils.

VENEZUELA

He whom God loves, his house is well known.

CHILE

❖

Let the unripe go with the ripe ones.

DOMINICAN REPUBLIC

❖

A man possesses beauty in his quality and a woman possesses quality in her beauty.

CUBA

❖

Face to face respect appears.

ECUADOR

❖

Once a bell is cracked it is never again made whole.

GUATEMALA

❖

Men meet, only mountains do not.

MEXICO

❖

Avarice is the only passion that never ages.

PUERTO RICO

❖

He who finds not love finds nothing.

COLOMBIA

❖

No one has done good who has not suffered disillusion-
ment.

NICARAGUA

❖

If there was not bad taste, goods would not be sold.

PANAMA

❖

A quarrel is like buttermilk, the more you stir it, the more
sour it grows.

BOLIVIA

❖

To be a merchant, the art consists more in recovering than
in making sales.

PERU

He who learns well defends himself well.

ARGENTINA

❖

Once is not often and twice is not always.

COSTA RICA

❖

A mother has little love for a son who did not give her pain.

VENEZUELA

❖

God does not wound with both hands.

CHILE

❖

It is not the load but the overload that kills.

DOMINICAN REPUBLIC

For the chaste woman, God suffices.

CUBA

❖

I will not jest with my eye or my faith.

COLOMBIA

❖

A good name conceals theft.

GUATEMALA

❖

For one loaf the covetous loses a hundred.

· MEXICO

❖

There is not the thickness of a peso between good and evil.

PUERTO RICO

May the sun set for me where I keep my love.

COLOMBIA

❖

A small spark makes a great fire.

PANAMA

❖

Diligence is the mother of good fortune.

BOLIVIA

❖

While one is gaining anything, one is losing nothing.

PERU

❖

The mind can make a heaven of hell or a hell of heaven.

COSTA RICA

God helps everyone with what is his own.

CHILE

❖

Nay contains the same number of letters as yea.

DOMINICAN REPUBLIC

❖

There is no better mirror than the face of an old friend.

CUBA

❖

God causes the good man's seed to flourish.

COLOMBIA

❖

Anger of the mind is poison to the soul.

ECUADOR

Even a hair makes its shadow on the ground.

GUATEMALA

❖

Avarice commonly occasions injury to the person who displays it.

MEXICO

❖

For a good appetite no bread is hard.

PUERTO RICO

❖

To love and be wise is impossible.

COLOMBIA

❖

In our glories our memories fail us.

PANAMA

❖

Who goes ill ends ill.

BOLIVIA

❖

Let every man mind his own business.

PERU

❖

He who has bad habits loses them late or never.

ARGENTINA

❖

Every word has three explanations and three interpretations.

COSTA RICA

The little birds have God for their caterer.

CHILE

❖

It is a fine thing to command, though it be only a herd of
cattle.

DOMINICAN REPUBLIC

❖

When a friend asks, there is no morrow.

CUBA

❖

Against God's wrath no house is strong.

COLOMBIA

❖

One misfortune calls another.

GUATEMALA

❖

Look at the man you serve and you will see how much you are esteemed.

MEXICO

❖

It is better to sweat than to sneeze.

PUERTO RICO

❖

God makes his sun to rise on the good and on the evil.

CUBA

❖

You seek a cat with three legs but you will always find four.

COLOMBIA

❖

There is no worse counselor than fear.

PANAMA

❖

Take away the cause and you take away the sin.

BOLIVIA

❖

A fertile field, if it does not rest, becomes sterile.

ARGENTINA

❖

The beauty of the man is in his intelligence and the intelligence of the woman is in her beauty.

BOLIVIA

❖

Many go for wool and come back shorn themselves.

DOMINICAN REPUBLIC

❖

Friends who know one another salute from afar.

CUBA

❖

To whom God wishes well, his home is sweet to him.

COLOMBIA

❖

Much disorder brings with it much order.

GUATEMALA

❖

No one can bind himself to perform the impossible.

MEXICO

❖

To know the disease is the beginning of the cure.

PUERTO RICO

❖

Even a leaf does not flutter on the tree without the will of God.

CUBA

❖

The thieving cow doesn't miss the gap.
COLOMBIA

❖

The leafy tree does not always give savory fruit.
PANAMA

❖

The righteous sometimes pay for sinners.
BOLIVIA

❖

The wedge, to be good, must be of the same wood.
ARGENTINA

❖

If you see me, I see you, and if you understand me, I understand you.

BOLIVIA

❖

Three, helping each other, will bear the burden of six.

CUBA

❖

Man proposes, God disposes.

COLOMBIA

❖

The thief thinks that all men are thieves.

MEXICO

❖

A mouth without teeth is like a mill without stones.

PUERTO RICO

❖

God will dawn and we shall prosper.

CUBA

❖

For every dog there is a leash.

COLOMBIA

❖

A card that never appears neither wins nor loses.

PANAMA

❖

He who plants a walnut tree does not expect to eat of the fruit.

MEXICO

❖

Heaven always favors good desires.

BOLIVIA

❖

It is better to be a fool than obstinate.

MEXICO

❖

You may light another's candle with your own without loss.

PUERTO RICO

❖

He who flings water into a jar spills more than he collects.
ARGENTINA

❖

He who marries prudence is the brother-in-law of peace.
BOLIVIA

❖

A man who is prepared has half won the battle.
CUBA

❖

God knows the truth, let it rest there.
COLOMBIA

❖

By the claw you may know the lion.
MEXICO

Health and mirth create beauty.

❖

Do not intermingle with what does not concern you.

❖

There is no road so level as to have no rough places.

❖

Everyone is as God made him and very often worse.

❖

Honors change manners.

He who sleeps too long in the morning, let him borrow
the pillow of a debtor.

PUERTO RICO

❖

A man without a home is like a bird without a nest.

ARGENTINA

❖

He who does not look ahead remains behind.

CUBA

❖

He who does not intend to pay is not troubled in making
his bargain.

MEXICO

❖

There is no pain that lasts a hundred years and no sick person who endures it.

PUERTO RICO

❖

Do not sell to your friend, nor buy corn of a rich man.

CUBA

❖

Whether the pitcher strike the stone or the stone the pitcher, the pitcher suffers.

PANAMA

❖

White lies are but the ushers to black ones.

BOLIVIA

❖

Not all haste is the daughter of imprudence, nor all delay that of cowardice.

PUERTO RICO

❖

Associate with good men and you will be one of them.

ARGENTINA

❖

Every war ends where it should begin.

CUBA

❖

He who asks a question does not err easily.

MEXICO

❖

Death is deaf and blind.

❖

Do not be too timid nor excessively confident.

CUBA

❖

He who is ignorant at home is ignorant abroad.

MEXICO

❖

It is better to èat bread with love than fowl with grief.

BOLIVIA

❖

Often nine secrets should be kept to oneself and the tenth not revealed.

PUERTO RICO

❖

The wise man never says, "I did not think."

CUBA

❖

Evil falls on him who goes to seek it.

MEXICO

❖

Never say "no" from pride or "yes" from weakness.

PUERTO RICO

❖

No one should boast until he has finished.

❖

One wolf does not bite another.

❖

Rise early and you will see; work and you will get wealth.

❖

Do not run into debt with a rich man, or promise anything to a poor one.

❖

Everyone is the son of his own works.

MEXICO

❖

She who desires to see desires also to be seen.

PUERTO RICO

❖

If every fool carried a stick, firewood would be scarce.

CUBA

❖

No man is worth more than another if he does no more than another.

PUERTO RICO

❖